CANADA

North Dakota

Minnesota

Wisconsin

South Dakota

Michigan

New Hampshire

Vermont

New York

Massachusetts

Rhode Island

Connecticut

Iowa

Pennsylvania

New Jersey

Nebraska

Illinois

Indiana

Ohio

Delaware

Maryland

Washington, D.C.

West Virginia

Kansas

Missouri

Kentucky

Virginia

North Carolina

Tennessee

Oklahoma

Arkansas

South Carolina

Texas

Alabama

Georgia

Mississippi

Louisiana

Florida

N

W E

S

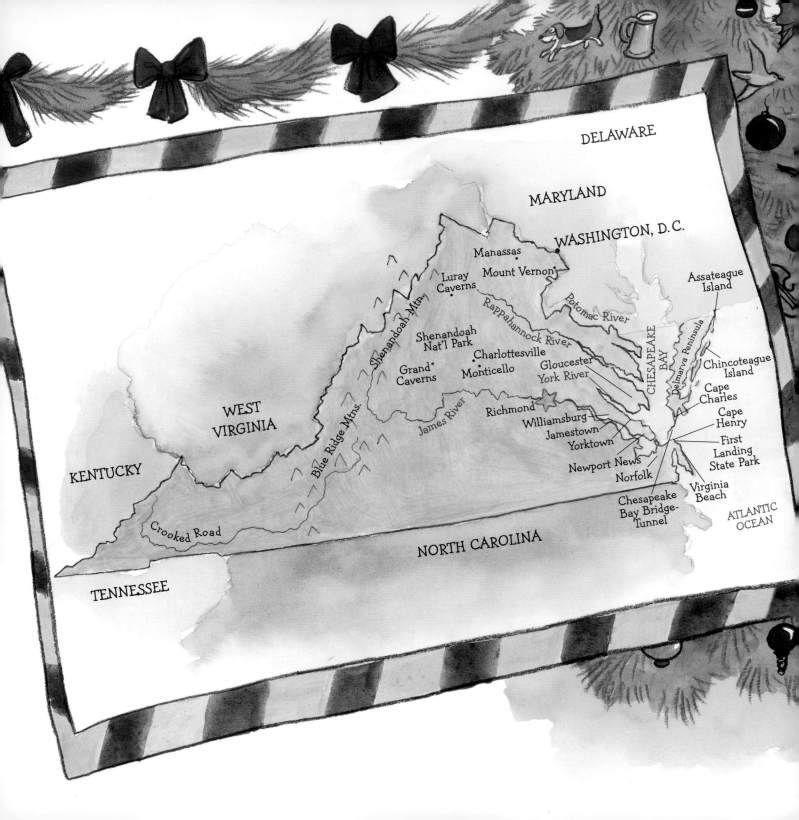

written by
Sue Corbett

illustrated by
Henry Cole

The Twelve Days of Christmas in Virginia

STERLING
New York / London

Dear Eleanor and William,

I can't believe your parents said yes! This is going to be the best winter break ever. Mom and I are planning a whole tour of Virginia. (We're hoping to show you how wonderful it is to live here so you will want to move closer to us!)

Bring clothes you can wear in layers—we have beaches and mountains, and the weather varies a lot.

Can't wait to see you both! Eleanor, I want to hear all about how the school play goes. I wish I could see you on stage as a skateboarding elf! William—take pictures!

Love,
Cousin Madison

Dear Eleanor,

We just got to Aunt Mary Jean's house from the airport. Madison was totally bummed about your broken leg, but is beaming "healing vibes" your way. (She is into meditation.) She thought it was a great idea to send you souvenirs from our travels. In fact, she said this could be a virtual tour, so you'll know exactly what you want to do when you get to come next time.

While Aunt M.J. made dinner (yummy ham biscuits and—gak!—peanut soup! I mean, it smelled good, but peanut soup?), Madison and I took these photos for you. According to Madison, (who may be something of a know-it-all), the northern cardinal is Virginia's state bird and—you might not be able to tell from the photo because it's winter—that's a dogwood, the state tree. A cardinal in a dogwood tree! Sure wish you were here . . .

More tomorrow.
Your only slightly freaked-out brother,

William

On the first day of Christmas,
my brother sent to me . . .

a cardinal in a
dogwood tree.

Dear Eleanor,

For my first day in Virginia, Madison decided to start at the beginning—First Landing State Park at the mouth of Chesapeake Bay, where Capt. Christopher Newport stepped ashore on April 26, 1607. (The bay's entrance is marked by Cape Henry and Cape Charles, named for King James's sons.) The crew then headed up the James River (named for guess who?) and founded Jamestown (not the most imaginative bunch, huh?), the first permanent English settlement in the New World.

Madison insisted we wade into the ocean and then walk back to shore, just like the first colonists probably did. ICY COLD! Madison declared, "I claim this beach for the kids of America!"

Cape Henry has two lighthouses: a stone one opened in 1792, and the "new" (1881!) black-and-white one. We climbed the old one, 191 steps to the lantern room—what a view! The keeper says it's even better in the summer, when you can look out and see dolphins and humpback whales!

Exploringly yours,
William

On the second day of Christmas,
my brother sent to me . . .

2 guiding lights

and a cardinal in a dogwood tree.

Ahoy, matey!

Sailed up to Jamestown today (on the highway—Aunt M.J. doesn't own a boat), where we boarded replicas of Capt. Newport's fleet. The ships look sturdy but small. The idea of spending four months crossing the Atlantic in the <u>Susan Constant</u>, wearing armor heavy enough to sink me on the spot, nearly made me seasick. Madison, however, climbed into the bosun's hammock and claimed the tide would rock her to sleep.

We learned about the Powhatan, native people who lived here when the English arrived. Madison pretended she was Pocahontas. I was the werowance (that's the Powhatan word for chief). We played quoits (a game like ring toss). I won. It is good to be chief.

At lunch, Aunt M.J. ordered crab cakes. I tried to picture what that could be—cakes made of crabs? With seaweed icing? Aunt M.J. insisted it was one of Virginia's most popular foods! Fortunately, even in pretend Colonial America, they serve cheeseburgers.

Your trying-to-be-adventurous-but-I-have-my-limits brother,
William

Eleanor,

Did you know that it's only 23 miles from the start of Colonial America to its end? That's the distance between Jamestown and Yorktown. Yorktown is where the Continental Army conquered the Redcoats in the last major battle of the Revolutionary War. After the defeat, General Cornwallis supposedly stayed in his tent and made somebody else surrender his sword. (Sore loser!)

Some people dressed in red coats and funny hats were reenacting Cornwallis's last stand. BOOM! BOOM! BOOM! BOOM! To save what was left of our hearing, we ducked into the gift shop, where we bought you a fife. Madison bought a white flag. I played your fife, chasing her over the hills the British built to keep the patriots from advancing. She surrendered without a fight.

Then we walked along the York River to see Gloucester on the far shore, where Cornwallis hoped to retreat to until a storm made the crossing impossible. We skipped stones and waved our flag at the boats drifting by.

Peace, sister,

William

Hi, Eleanor,

Today we went to Colonial Williamsburg, named for me. (Ha, ha.) On Duke of Gloucester Street, we met Madison's friends, Olivia and Sam, dressed in old-fashioned clothes. They showed us where we could get costumes, too. Madison pulled on a mob cap and I grabbed a tricorn hat. "Hurry up!" Sam said. "Governor Jefferson is speaking at the Capitol!" (An actor playing Thomas Jefferson, of course.) "Why 'Governor Jefferson'?" I asked. "It's 1779," Sam said. "We haven't won the war yet."

While we were all listening to Jefferson, Olivia spotted a lady in a full apron, headed toward us. "Hide! Grandmother Geddy is looking for help with the laundry," Olivia whispered. We ran to the Public Gaol (where Blackbeard's crew was once jailed), but Grandma caught us and put Olivia and Sam in the pillory.

After our imprisonment, Aunt M.J. sprang for mugs of apple cider at a tavern where Washington once dined. The cider smelled like cinnamon—yum. We clanked our mugs and wished you were here so we could put you in the pillory!

Miss you,
William

Dear Eleanor,

You've got to read the book *Misty of Chincoteague*. Aunt M. T. put on the audiobook version for the drive to Charlottesville. It's about two kids and ponies that <u>swim</u>, set right here in Virginia!

As you head west, the hills on the horizon really are blue—the Blue Ridge Mountains. We stopped at Monticello, home of Thomas Jefferson, one of EIGHT U.S. presidents born in Virginia. Jefferson's house is full of all the awesome stuff he collected. Can you imagine Mom putting a mastodon's jawbone on display in the front hall? He installed dumbwaiters (to bring food from the cellar kitchen to the dining room), and a two-pen machine that made an identical copy of whatever he was writing. (When you're writing the Declaration of Independence, a copy comes in handy.) After the tour, the guides taught us how to roll hoops with a stick. It's harder than it looks!

We didn't want to leave until we remembered that when we got in the car we'd hear more about the wild ponies of Chincoteague.

Get that book!

William

On the sixth day of Christmas, my brother sent to me . . .

6 hoops a-rolling

5 pewter mugs, 4 cannon blasts, 3 tall ships, 2 guiding lights, and a cardinal in a dogwood tree.

Woo-hoo! Aunt M.J. said we needed a break (no pun intended—how's your leg?) from history. I didn't realize it until she said it but this is the most EDUCATIONAL vacation I've ever had. So we hit the slopes! Madison had never been on a 'board before. I helped her on the bunny hill until she caught on. She only biffed badly twice. She said she's ready to learn tricks next time. I did a 360 off the jump and I think she was impressed.

Next we're headed to a party at Bert's. He is a friend of Aunt M.J.'s, a fiddler who lives along the Crooked Road. I wonder whether crooked is different from curvy because the road up the mountain slithered like a snake. Aunt M.J. put on <u>Misty</u>, but after skiing all day, I felt like my eyelids were carrying weights, and the next thing I knew it was pitch dark and Aunt M.J. was shaking me awake at Bert's cabin.

Zzzzzzz,
William

Eleanor—Sing to the tune of that famous New Year's song,
Auld Lang Syne, but with a TWANG!

I stirred a pot of Brunswick stew,
M.J. made her fried cornbread.
Eight fiddlers strummed, me and Maddy hummed,
then danced until day's end.

Along the Crooked Road, ol' Sis,
there's music everywhere.
Along the Crooked Road, ol' Sis,
how we wished that you were there . . .

Happy New Year! See you soon!
William and Madison

P.S. The music all along the Crooked Road is called
bluegrass, but I've seen the grass and it's green. Maybe
they should call it blue mountain music?

Eleanor,

Today's stop was way cool! We went to a cave (Virginia has thousands) where troops lived during the Civil War—some soldiers even signed their names on the walls! It's called Grand Caverns.

Our guide, Otto, gave us flashlights. We were the only people on his tour. "We get more critters than people this time of year," he told us. This would be a good place to visit in August—it's always 54 degrees underground.

Madison impressed Otto by knowing the difference between the formations on the floor and the ones above us: "Stalactites hang on TIGHT. Stalagmites MIGHT reach up to the ceiling." Otto called her "a natural spelunker."

Madison looked confused. For once I knew something she didn't! "That's a cave explorer," I explained.

We turned off our flashlights to see how dark it was. Spooky! When we turned them back on, a swarm of bats flew down from the stalactites! Madison's eyes got wide. "We coexist with the animals that were here first," Otto said.

See what I mean by way cool?

xo,

William

On the ninth day of Christmas,
my brother sent to me . . .

9 bats a-swooping

8 fiddlers fiddling, **7** boarders shredding,
6 hoops a-rolling, **5** pewter mugs, **4** cannon blasts,
3 tall ships, **2** guiding lights,
and a cardinal in a dogwood tree.

Dear Eleanor,

Our next stop was Mount Vernon, home of George Washington, on the Potomac River. There is still a farm with hogs, sheep, oxen, and horses. There were also bowls on the ground with water in them, even inside the buildings.

"For our canine visitors," a guide explained. "We always welcome dogs here, and today the local chapter of the Foxhound Society is meeting on the Bowling Green."

"Virginia's state dog!" Madison said.

"Correct," the guide told us. "Washington bred his English hunting dogs with French bluetick hounds given to him by the Marquis de Lafayette, so he is credited with creating the breed now known as the American Foxhound."

We raced over to the lawn outside Washington's mansion and there they were—the four-legged descendents of dogs owned by the Father of Our Country!

xox,
William

P.S. If you are up to the part in <u>Misty</u> where the man from Norfolk buys Phantom, don't worry. Just keep reading!

Dear Eleanor,

We were caught up in the end of <u>Misty</u>, so neither of us wondered about our next stop till we both saw the sign: WELCOME TO CHINCOTEAGUE ISLAND.

We couldn't believe it! We crossed a bridge from Chincoteague to Assateague Island and got a map from the visitor center. We hiked to a viewing area overlooking a grazing field. We drove around slowly, even onto the beach, taking turns with the binoculars. There was lots of ocean, but no ponies.

"You'll just have to come again, William," Aunt M.J. said.

We stopped to eat back on Chincoteague. M.J. got oysters. (They look like something you would spit out, not swallow.) Madison asked the waitress if the ponies were just a story.

"Oh, they're real. Why?" the waitress asked. Aunt M.J. explained.

The waitress said she'd make a call and came back, smiling. "If you've got time, Captain Tom can take you to see them." His boat pulled up behind the restaurant. He knew right where the ponies were. They were running races!

Wow!

William

On the eleventh day of Christmas,
my brother sent to me . . .

11 ponies racing

10 puppies chasing, 9 bats a-swooping,
8 fiddlers fiddling, 7 boarders shredding,
6 hoops a-rolling, 5 pewter mugs,
4 cannon blasts, 3 tall ships, 2 guiding lights,
and a cardinal in a dogwood tree.

Dear Eleanor,

We drove back along the skinny Virginia Peninsula, crossing the Chesapeake Bay Bridge-Tunnel, which has to be the longest trip in the world across the water without a boat, from Cape Charles to Cape Henry. Madison wanted to find you some seashells, so we went to Virginia Beach. It was just us and the birds—big black-hooded seagulls and tiny dancing birds called plovers. The ocean looked steel gray and cold. Madison didn't suggest we wade in this time.

I'm packing now, but SOME of your gifts won't fit in my suitcase. You'll just have to see them when you, Mom, and Dad pick me up at the airport. My luggage weighs a ton. The soup cans alone make it too heavy to lift. See, when we stopped for lunch there was peanut soup on the menu and I thought, what the heck? I was cold. It was hot. And you know what? I bought you some because it tastes as good as it smells! You HAVE to try it.

See you very soon!
William

On the twelfth day of Christmas,
my brother sent to me . . .

12 plovers looping

11 ponies racing, 10 puppies chasing,
9 bats a-swooping, 8 fiddlers fiddling, 7 boarders shredding,
6 hoops a-rolling, 5 pewter mugs, 4 cannon blasts,
3 tall ships, 2 guiding lights,
and a cardinal in a dogwood tree.

Virginia: The Old Dominion

Capital: Richmond · **State abbreviation:** VA · **Largest city:** Virginia Beach · **State bird:** the northern cardinal · **State flower and tree:** the dogwood · **State dog:** the American foxhound · **State dance:** the square dance · **State insect:** the tiger swallowtail butterfly · **State fish:** the brook trout · **State motto:** "Sic Semper Tyrannis" ("Thus Always to Tyrants")

Some Famous Virginians:

William Clark (1770–1838) and **Meriwether Lewis** (1774–1809) were native Virginians selected by President Thomas Jefferson to lead the Northwest Expedition, an exploratory journey begun in 1804, across the American continent in search of a route to the Pacific Ocean.

Nikki Giovanni (1943–) is an acclaimed poet, essayist, and teacher. She has been a member of the faculty at Virginia Tech in Blacksburg since 1987, where she is now a Distinguished Professor of English. She is the author of more than two dozen books.

Patrick Henry (1736–1799) is famous for saying, "Give me liberty, or give me death," to show his commitment to self-governance for the American colonies. He served two terms as Virginia's governor.

Christopher Newport (1561–1617) captained the *Susan Constant*, one of three ships that arrived in Jamestown in 1607, establishing the first permanent English settlement in North America. Christopher Newport University in Newport News was named in his honor.

Amedeo Obici (1877–1947) emigrated from Italy to Pennsylvania in the 1880s, but left his biggest legacy in Suffolk, Virginia, where he moved in the early 1920s to oversee his growing peanut empire, the Planters Peanut Company. A statue of Mr. Peanut stands in town.

Mary Peake (1823–1862) taught former slaves to read and write under the shade of an oak tree in Hampton. This spot was the site of the first Southern reading of President Abraham Lincoln's Emancipation Proclamation, which abolished slavery. The Emancipation Oak still stands, designated as one of the 10 Great Trees of the World.

Booker T. Washington (1856–1915) was a slave whose owners encouraged his education. After emancipation from slavery, he took his savings and walked from Roanoke to Hampton to enroll at Hampton Institute (now Hampton University). He so excelled at school that he was hired as a teacher, and later went on to found the Tuskegee Institute in Tuskegee, Alabama.

STERLING and the distinctive Sterling logo are
registered trademarks of Sterling Publishing Co,. Inc

Library of Congress Cataloging-in-Publication Data

Corbett, Sue.
The twelve days of Christmas in Virginia / by Sue Corbett ; illustrated by Henry Cole.
p. cm.
ISBN 978-1-4027-6344-1
1. Virginia--Juvenile literature. 2. Virginia--Geography--Juvenile literature.
3. Virginia--History, Local--Juvenile literature. 4. Counting--Juvenile literature.
I. Cole, Henry, 1955- ill. II. Title.
F226.3.C67 2009
975.5--dc22   2008043109

6 8 10 9 7 5
05/17

Published by Sterling Publishing Co., Inc.
387 Park Avenue South, New York, NY 10016
Text copyright © 2009 by Sue Corbett
Illustrations copyright © 2009 by Henry Cole
The original illustrations for this book were created in acrylics and colored pencil.
Distributed in Canada by Sterling Publishing
c/o Canadian Manda Group, 165 Dufferin Street
Toronto, Ontario, Canada M6K 3H6
Distributed in the United Kingdom by GMC Distribution Services
Castle Place, 166 High Street, Lewes, East Sussex, England BN7 1XU
Distributed in Australia by Capricorn Link (Australia) Pty. Ltd.
P.O. Box 704, Windsor, NSW 2756, Australia

Designed by Kate Moll and Patrice Sheridan

Misty of Chincoteague was originally published by Rand McNally, Chicago, 1947. All rights reserved.
Mr. Peanut® is a registered trademark of Kraft Foods Global, Inc., Northfield, IL 60026. All rights reserved.

Sterling ISBN 978-1-4027-6344-1

For information about custom editions, special sales, premium and
corporate purchases, please contact Sterling Special Sales
Department at 800-805-5489 or specialsales@sterlingpublishing.com.

For Brigit, my Virginia belle —S.C.
For K.W.E. —H.C.